JESS AND THE STINKY COWBOYS

by Janice Lee Smith
pictures by Lisa Thiesing

DIAL BOOKS FOR YOUNG READERS
New York

Dedicated with all my love to:
Mark R. Joseph and Annie "Tigger" McPeters
—J. L. S.

To Chrissy
—L. T.

Published by Dial Books for Young Readers
A division of Penguin Young Readers Group
345 Hudson Street
New York, New York 10014
Text copyright © 2004 by Janice Lee Smith
Pictures copyright © 2004 by Lisa Thiesing
All rights reserved
Manufactured in China on acid-free paper
The Dial Easy-to-Read logo
is a registered trademark of Dial Books for Young Readers,
a division of Penguin Group (USA) Inc.
®TM 1,162,718.
1 3 5 7 9 10 8 6 4 2

Library of Congress Cataloging-in-Publication Data
Smith, Janice Lee, date.
Jess and the stinky cowboys / by Janice Lee Smith ;
pictures by Lisa Thiesing.
p.   cm.
Summary: When a band of stinky cowboys who refuse to bathe
comes to town while the sheriff is away, young Deputy Jess and her aunt,
Deputy Gussy, must find a way to enforce the No-Stink law.
ISBN 0-8037-2641-4
[1. Cleanliness—Fiction. 2. Peace officers—Fiction.
3. Cowboys—Fiction. 4. Baths—Fiction.
5. Frontier and pioneer life—West (U.S.)—Fiction.
6. West (U.S.)—Fiction. 7. Tall tales.] I. Thiesing, Lisa, ill. II. Title.
PZ7.S6499 Je 2004
[Fic]—dc21   2002011886

Reading Level 2.3

The art was created using watercolors,
colored pencil, and ink.

CONTENTS

THE STINKERS!

Two deputies rocked in their chairs
on the jailhouse porch.

"Snake Gulch is as quiet as a flea,"
Deputy Gussy told Deputy Jess.

"I've known noisy fleas," said Jess.

Jess's dad was the town's sheriff.

He was chasing outlaws

in the Very Bad Lands.

Jess and her aunt Gussy were in charge

until he got back.

"We have been busy since Dad left,"

Jess said to Gussy.

"We have stopped bank robbers,

a cattle stampede,

and a spelling bee."

"That bee was a mistake," said Gussy.

"Those spellers were rowdy!" said Jess.

"Anyway, I like a quiet spell."

It didn't last long.

Suddenly, a cattle drive came to town.

Its smell knocked the two deputies

clean off their rockers.

"I've never smelled cows like that!"

Jess told Gussy.

"I know that stink," Gussy declared.

"It's not the cows. It's the cowboys!"

Jess followed the cattle up Main Street.

She had to hold her nose to talk.

"I don't want to hurt your feelings,"

she told the cowboys,

"but you smell worse than your cows."

"Thank you!" said Hairy Larry.

"We have a No-Stink law," said Jess.

"All you cowboys must take a bath.

They cost just five cents at the hotel."

"You can buy candy and root beer

for five cents!" yelled Larry.

"Besides, who gets to decide

if something stinks enough

to break that law?" asked Flea-Bit Fred.

"I do," Jess told him. "I'm the deputy.

And I say the way you smell

is a crime!"

THE STINK CLOUD

"No baths today!" yelled Larry.

"No baths tomorrow!" shouted Fred.

"No baths ever!" roared all the cowboys.

13

So Jess put them all in jail.

"It smells worse in this jail

than a cow pie in July!" Gussy said.

"I will move the cowboys

under the oak tree," Jess told Gussy.

"There is a strong breeze there."

Jess herded the cowboys outside

and drew a circle in the dirt.

"This is your new jail cell," she said.

"You can't go outside the circle."

"That's not fair!" said Fred.

"You have to stay here

until you take baths," Jess told him.

"Or until it rains and washes you off."

The sky was clear and blue.

There was just one little brown cloud.

It was right above the cowboys.

Then the stink cloud grew bigger.

Mayor Mike called a town meeting

to decide what to do.

"Throw those smelly varmints

in the horse tank!" yelled Barber Bob.

"Bad for the horses," said Mayor Mike.

"Toss those stinky rascals in the river!"

shouted Grocer Gertie.

"Bad for the fish," said Mayor Mike.

"Then I will have a sale on baths,"

said Hotel Hank.

"They are only two and a half cents."

"Bad for us cowboys," said Larry.

"But I will throw in extra bubbles,"

said Hotel Hank.

"I will even scrub your back

with a cactus brush."

"No baths today!" yelled Larry.

"No baths tomorrow!" shouted Fred.

"No baths ever!" roared all the cowboys.

Night came and the stink cloud stayed.

The cowboys sat around a campfire.

First they sang "Great Green Gobs

of Greasy Grimy Gopher Guts."

Then they sang "When You Wish

Upon a Cow."

Jess took pillows out to the cowboys.

"I miss my mom," Fred told her.

"Boo-hoo!" cried Larry.

"I miss my horse."

"I didn't know cowboys cried,"

said Jess.

"They cry," he told her.

"They just don't take baths."

STINK TOWN

"The flies and buzzards left

this morning," Gussy told Jess.

"Even the stinkbugs won't stay."

Mayor Mike called a new town meeting.

"This stink is as mean as a snake

and twice as much trouble," he said.

"No one wants to stay

in this stinky town," said Hotel Hank.

"So baths for cowboys are now free!"

"No baths today!" yelled Larry.

"No baths tomorrow!" shouted Fred.

"No baths ever!" roared all the cowboys.

"I have a great idea," said the mayor.

"We will build a giant windmill.

It will blow the stink cloud away."

"I hope it blows the cowboys away too!"

yelled Barber Bob.

"Now that's just rude!" said Fred.

Everyone in town pitched in
to build the giant windmill.

"Do you think this will work?"

Jess asked Gussy.

"We'll know soon," said Gussy.

Two strong mules helped spin the windmill
faster and faster.

"Yahoo-a-roo!" yelled the cowboys.

They held on tight to the oak tree.

But the stink cloud did not move a bit.

The windmill began to shake.

First it leaned one way.

Then it leaned the other.

"Run away!" yelled Barber Bob.

SCREECH! SCRUNCH! CRASH!

The windmill fell to the ground.

And the stink cloud grew even bigger.

"Uh-oh!" said Jess.

"Uh-oh!" said Mayor Mike.

"Uh-oh!" said Grocer Gertie.

The stink cloud began to spit

great big gobs of greasy goo.

"Whose goofy idea was it to build

that goofy windmill anyway?"

asked Mayor Mike.

STOPPING THE STINK

The stink cloud grew until it

covered the sky over Snake Gulch.

Jess took a walk around town.

She was trying to come up with an idea.

31

She walked past the river.

The fish were crying.

She walked past Matchstick Mort,

the fire chief.

And suddenly. . . Jess had an idea!

"Listen!" Jess told Gussy.

"I know just what to do!"

CLANG! CLANG! CLANG!

Gussy rode up in the fire wagon.

"Yikes!" yelled Larry.

"Where's the fire?"

First Jess hooked the fire hose

to the water tank.

"This doesn't look good," said Larry.

Next Gussy poured soap flakes, shampoo,

and rose perfume into the water tank.

"This looks downright bad," said Fred.

Then Jess aimed the hose

at the cowboys. . . .

"Get ready for bath time!" she yelled.

"Run for your lives!" yelled Larry.

WHOOSH! SPURT! SPLOOSH!

The water sent the cowboys tumbling.

SLIP! SLIDE! SPLAT!

Cowboys slid everywhere.

Larry crashed into Mayor Mike.

They both floated past Jess

on a stream of bubbles.

"Yahoo!" yelled Larry.

"Yahoo too!" yelled Mayor Mike.

The stink cloud became a bit smaller.

Barber Bob threw a lasso around Larry.

"Time for a haircut," said Bob.

Hotel Hank swam after Fred.

"Time for a scrub," said Hank.

The stink cloud became much smaller.

Gussy rounded up the cattle.

"We'll wash the cows too," she said.

"Don't forget my horse," yelled Larry.

The stink cloud went "Poof!"

And it was gone for good.

"Hooray! Yippee!" cheered the people.

"I saved the town!" cheered Mayor Mike.

"I will now offer this kind of bath

to my guests!" said Hotel Hank.

"We could change our name to

Bubble Bath Gulch!" said Barber Bob.

"Without all that stink,

you're sort of cute," Gussy told Larry.

Two deputies rocked in their chairs

on the jailhouse porch.

"Snake Gulch is as quiet as a flea,"

Deputy Gussy told Deputy Jess.

"I've known noisy fleas," Jess said.

They looked around.

Main Street was soaking wet.

The buzzards, the flies,

and even the stinkbugs were back.

Every cow and cowboy was clean.

So was Larry's horse.

The town smelled like rose perfume.

And there wasn't a cloud in sight.

Jess's dad came riding into town.

He had a wagon full of crabby outlaws.

Gussy took them into the jail.

"This is the best-smelling town

we've ever been in," Bad Bill told her.

"It smells just lovely,"

said Worse Walt.

"The town really does smell great!"

said Sheriff Dad. "Well . . . mostly."

"What do you mean?" asked Jess.

"Let's just say it's a good thing
it is Saturday," said her dad.
"And Saturday is bath night."
Jess looked up.
A small stink cloud was forming
right above her head.

"*I* have an idea," said Larry.

He was holding the fire hose.

"This doesn't look good," said Jess.

"And *I* want to help," said Fred.

"We *all* do!" said the cowboys.

"In fact, it looks downright bad,"

said Jess.

"Yahoo-a-roo!" yelled the cowboys.

SPURT! SPRAY! SPLOOSH!

Jess's bath time began—

with a splash!